THE
BRUMMSTEIN

THE
BRUMMSTEIN

PETER
ADOLPHSEN

TRANSLATED FROM THE DANISH BY
CHARLOTTE BARSLUND

PUBLISHED BY

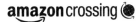

The Brummstein by Peter Adolphsen was first published in 2003 by
Samleren in Denmark as *Brummstein*.

Translated from the Danish by Charlotte Barslund.
First published in English in 2011 by AmazonCrossing.

Published by AmazonCrossing
P.O. Box 400818
Las Vegas, NV 89140

ISBN-13: 9781611090284
ISBN-10: 1611090288
LCCN: 2011900974

THANK YOU TO:

Allan Hansen, Charlotte Christensen, Christiane Müller, Jørgen Olesen, Litteraturrådet, Per Øhrgaard, Ruth Heyn-Johnsen, Statens Kunstfond, Steffen Hahn, and Uwe Englert.

The constant orogeny of the Alps is caused by the breakup of the microcontinent Adria from Africa in the Jurassic, its subsequent rotation over the then existing Tethys Sea, and its collision with Eurasia; if we apply the famous metaphor which depicts the Earth's age as a calendar year, when dinosaurs become extinct on Boxing Day, hominids emerge on New Year's Eve, and when, at the time of writing, ten seconds have passed since the Roman Empire's five seconds expired, then these events took place on December 19 and 23 respectively. In the West, the process of comprehending this vast expanse of time commenced just one and a half geological seconds ago with the publication in 1788 of James Hutton's *Theory of the Earth* with its frequently quoted line: "No vestige of a beginning, no prospect of an end." Shortly before that in the year 1650, James Ussher, Archbishop of Armagh, had dated the completion of creation to Sunday, October 23, 4004 BC, based on his analysis of Biblical sources, the Hebrew calendar, and astronomical calculations.

Today, however, in the era of radiometric dating, we are confident that creation began approximately 4.6 billion years ago—a period of time so immense that metaphors such as a single calendar year must serve as crutches for our thoughts.

Mark Twain resorted to another image: if the full height of the Eiffel Tower represents the Earth's age, then the human race appears as the final coat of paint on the knob at the very top is applied. The journalist with the toothbrush moustache went on to ask the logical follow-up question, but he was, however, reluctant to answer it: Was the tower built for the sole purpose of applying this one coat of paint? "I dunno." In an age where we seem to have acknowledged the purposelessness of our species, it's tempting nevertheless to stress this anthropocentric view of being at the very top. An early proponent of this purposelessness was Friedrich Nietzsche, some nine years younger than Twain, who wrote about intelligent animals, on a planet in a remote corner of countless solar systems' flickering grains of sand, which must die out when nature takes a shallow breath and freezes their planet:

> "One might invent such a fable and
> still not have illustrated sufficiently

how wretched, how shadowy and tran-
sient, how aimless and arbitrary, the
human intellect appears in nature...
Could we but communicate with the
moth, then we would understand that
it, too, flies through the air with this
pathos and feels the flying center of
the world within itself."

Prompted by poor health and the medicinal imper-
atives of his time, the philosopher with the walrus
moustache was a frequent guest at the Sils-Maria
health resort in the Swiss Alps, which neither then
nor since have ceased to grow under visiting feet: as
much as two millimeters for every non-metaphorical
calendar year, mainly at Chur in the Graubünden
Canton as Adria grinds its way into the lithosphere
and buries itself in the bed of the Tethys Sea.

Twenty to thirty million years ago in real time
and approximately two days in the metaphorical
downscaling, the plates of Adria and Europe con-
verged and the lower crust of the former was forced
so deeply into the latter that it split. The dislodged
lower crust grew heavier as a result of metamorphic
conversion and continued to sink. At the same time,
a roughly 0.7 cubic kilometer large massif of Adria's

crystalline base broke off, but rather than follow suit into the hot abyss under Europe, it traveled upwards through layers of limestone and can today be found close to the Earth's surface encased in the 2,314-meter-high Mount Silberen, thirty-seven kilometers west-northwest of Chur. This rain-furrowed mountain contains Hölloch, estimated to be the world's fourth-largest cave system. In a tunnel called Tauchstrecke the water slowly washed away the surrounding limestone to reveal a corner of the aforementioned small massif. Here, unheard by any-one except two people at either end of the twenti-eth century, is a constant humming caused by the crystal structure of this repeatedly metamorphosed massif which acts as a resonator for particular com-binations of sound waves triggered by millions of earthquakes that accompanied the formation of the Alps. A few specimens of the five species of *Niphargus* genus found in Hölloch can also detect the vibra-tions in their antennae and the sensitive hairs on their bodies.

The tectonic compression of approximately sixty thousand hectares of seabed to a quarter produced numerous folds and faults. Millions of years of Tethys Sea sediment, now in the form of limestone mountains, shot several kilometers into the air and so became exposed to the erosion and corrosion of rain, snow, and ice, that is mechanical wear and chemical dissolution. Approximately one million years ago, roughly two hours of the geological "year," water started to form the Silberen System, the oldest part of the Muota Valley Caves, though officially it has yet to be declared a part of Hölloch as by the year 2002 speleologists had yet to discover the passage which links the cave systems. Several dye tests, however, have shown that water has found a way through.

Humans don't appear to have discovered the caves until 1875 when a gangly and gray-bearded mountain farmer called Alois Ulrich found the entrance to the geologically youngest section of the caves, known today as the Basic System. Other early cave explorers include the town clerk Melchior Bürgler and the painter Josef Leonhard Betschart, who together ventured as far as Böser Wand in the 1880s, but the name Hans Julius Widmer-Osterwalder is particularly associated with Hölloch because this Zurich engineer and glazier lived and died trying to make these wonderful dripstone caves accessible to the public. Ever since he and his wife Hermine first visited Hölloch in 1899, Widmer had fantasized about the tourist potential of the caves, and in 1902 he bought the plot of land which encompassed the entrance to the caves. After considerable difficulty in attracting investors, he finally convinced a Belgian syndicate to invest. They formed the company, Grottes de Muotathal (Höllloch) en Suisse, in 1905 with a share capital of one million Belgian francs. Soon afterwards more than one hundred workers and engineers started building walkways, enlarging bottlenecks with explosives, and installing electric lights in 1,006 meters of the caves. To divert the summer torrents of melted snow from the caves, they attempted to drill a tunnel in from the outside to give the Hölloch stream a direct outlet to the Schlichenden Brunnen River, but efforts were abandoned after seven laborious and costly horizontal meters into the solid rock face. Instead they constructed concrete walls inside the caves to contain the water. The relatively luxurious, forty-room Hôtel des Grottes was also built in the expectation of many visitors, but the high entry fee and the difficulties of reaching the remote valley kept them away; the investors fled with the remaining capital, and Hans Widmer died a ruined and broken man in 1909. The destruction of many walkways and walls as well as the electrical installation, the pinnacle of the achievements of the Hölloch workers, by a flash flood in June 1910 dealt the venture the final blow. In the years that followed, local peasant boys smashed every window of the abandoned Hôtel des Grottes.

However, before it came to this sorry state, Josef and Andrea Siedler had been two of the few guests to stay at the hotel. Josef, a deputy director of the Ausburg branch of Gothaer Life Insurance Bank, had come to Hölloch to find the entrance to the underworld. He was convinced that the Earth's mantle embraced a gigantic vacuum, an idea that wasn't regarded as scientifically refuted at the time; on the contrary, the Austrian geologist Eduard Suess, in his three-volume work *The Face of the Earth* (1883–1909), had argued authoritatively for the contraction theory, which explains the formation of the Earth's current surface by horizontal traction in the mantle that occurs when its inner masses contract as they cool. To illustrate his theory, Suess used an apple whose skin wrinkles as it dries from its core. Josef had himself carefully halved a dried apple and revealed a vacuum between its peel and its flesh. It was there, he believed, between the mantle and the Earth's contracting core that the subterranean or intra-terranean race would be found.

There were numerous other and rather conflicting testimonies to this vacuum and creatures ranging from the ominous warning in Isaiah 2:21 "to go into the clefts of the rocks, and into the tops of the ragged rocks, for fear of the Lord" to the Tibetan legend of Agharti, a subterranean ideal state, the Akkadian Aralu, a castle behind seven ramparts in a gigantic cave, and Edward Bulwer-Lytton's 1871 novel, *The Coming Race.* Josef, in his capacity as a corresponding member of the Berlin Vril Society, had particular faith in the latter. Admittedly, Bulwer-Lytton, the author of a series of novels of which the best known was *The Last Days of Pompeii* (1834), had claimed that his story of a subterranean race of supermen was pure fiction, but Josef and his kindred spirits believed that Bulwer-Lytton was well aware that anyone making such claims in earnest would expose himself to ridicule and ultimately confinement to an institution.

The anonymous narrator in *The Coming Race* is a wealthy young traveler who ventures down a newly constructed mineshaft and discovers the entrance to a world inhabited by the Vril-yas. During the Flood this people fled to the hollow interior of the Earth where they have created a civilization which far surpasses that of the humans on the surface. With small sticks they control the Vril power, described as "the unity in natural energetic agencies." The narrator is reminded of the English physicist Michael Faraday, who imagined that:

> "the various forms under which the forces of matter are made manifest, have one common origin; or, in other words, are so directly related and mutually dependent, that they are convertible, as it were into one another, and possess equivalents of power in their action."

The friendly Vril-ya, in whose house the traveler is staying, explains that Vril power is much more than the sum total of the natural forces known to surface humans. He proceeds to lecture his visitor on trance and telepathy, which regrettably exceeds the imagination of his listener. The young man, who is never permitted to handle a Vril stick as he would undoubtedly cause an accident, describes it as follows:

"It is hollow and has in the handle several stops, keys, or springs by which its force can be altered, modified, or directed—so that by one process it destroys, by another it heals—by one it affects bodies, and by another it can exercise a certain influence over minds. It is usually carried in the convenient size of a walking staff, but it has slides by which it can be lengthened or shortened at will."

He adds that destructive Vril power can be stored in containers which can be fired five to six hundred English miles and "reduce to ashes...a capital twice as vast as London."

Josef understood perfectly the power that possessing such a weapon would bestow and believed it to be imperative to do what he could to prevent it from falling into the wrong hands. He knew the surface people's hunger for discovery was inevitably twinned with their lust for power, and it was simply a matter of time before it would be too late. In the event that the Vril-yas, provoked by the intrusive humans, chose to invade the Earth, he, the insignificant Josef Siedler from the small town of Ausburg, would be only too pleased to serve as a friendly ambassador. Consequently, his heart skipped a beat one morning when he read the following headline in his daily *Allgemeine Zeitung*:

THE ENTRANCE TO THE UNDERWORLD IS OPENED

The story concerned the official opening of the Hölloch Caves on July 1, 1906. Next to a picture of the Dolomite Hall it was reported that although only one kilometer of the caves had been made accessible to the public, the cave explorer Hans Widmer, who was the driving force behind the project, knew of even deeper caves. "No one knows how deep Hölloch goes," he declared. "We joke that it reaches all the way to hell, but of course we know it doesn't really."

"You're wrong on two counts," Josef whispered to himself. "The caves go all the way down, but there's no hell at the bottom." A poem composed by the local rhymester, Richard Hardmeier, in honor of the occasion was printed below the picture:

> Now open, gate to hell,
> And show us your terrors
> Such as we have never seen before

In wide open spaces.
As yet there is no road, no path,
And barely had your trail been found
Before a few, brimming with courage,
Quenched their thirst for knowledge
    in you.
Many people wished to see
The wonders behind your mountain
    door,
But only a few could enter,
So paths were built.
And so that no one would get lost,
Electric light now fills you;
Soon songs of praise will echo
Throughout your wide halls.

Josef recited the poem in a sonorous voice to Andrea, who dropped her embroidery onto her lap in order to give it her full attention.

In November of the following year they finally traveled to Hölloch. After a rather punishing journey through Bregenz, Zurich, and Schwyz where it snowed constantly, the couple took a room at the

Hôtel des Grottes. Over breakfast the next morning they discovered that the only other guests at the hotel were a couple of young honeymooners from Innsbruck, of rather modest birth and income as Andrea remarked when they were alone once more. *"Ulula cum lupis, cum quibus esse cupis"* (Whoever keeps company with wolves, will learn to howl), replied Josef, who regarded himself as well-read.

Later, as the newlyweds clearly preferred their own company, Andrea and Josef undertook the four-hour tour of the expanded sections of the caves where their guide, a young man who introduced himself as Udo, courteously explained the mysteries of the dripstone caves.

"These wonderful rock formations were created by the persistent dripping over several millennia. In ancient times people believed the dripstones to be anything from congealed water or strange creatures in a state between the mineral and plant kingdom to lost souls condemned to immobility or even demons rising from hell. The latter hypothesis was proposed in 1689 by Johann Weichard Valvasor, who had visited the Adelsberger Cave in Slovenia. Hölloch was, as the lady and gentleman might know, discovered only thirty-two years ago. But let us return to the dripstones: Today we know that they're formed when surface water trickles down and transports with it microscopic amounts of limestone, decomposed soil, and plant material, if any such is present. And we just happen to find ourselves underneath the primeval Bödmeren Forest."

His last words were delivered in a somber tone and accompanied by a dramatic pointing to the ceiling of the cave. Andrea shuddered theatrically, mainly to reward the guide, whom she found rather sweet. Josef noticed this, but he was unaware of its significance and confused it with a slightly stiff neck. They walked on.

"Dripstones are usually composed of calcium carbonate, more rarely of silicic acid also known as chalcedony, or of hydrated iron (III) oxide-hydroxide, also known as limonite," Udo continued, having assured himself that his guests were keeping up. "When dissolved, these substances travel with the precipitation and meltwater as it seeps down to the ceiling of the cave. If the water drips very slowly, solid microscopic remains are left hanging from the ceiling, first as a small, wart-shaped growth that eventually grows to the sizes and shapes you see here through a continuous supply of material from water trickling down or evaporating from the dripstone. Sometimes the water gouges a channel in the core of the dripstone though which it travels to reach the tip. If more water is present than can evaporate from the surface of the dripstone, the excess will drip and form a dripstone growing upwards that may ultimately join with the dripstone hanging from the ceiling. A hanging dripstone is called a stalactite; the upright one a stalagmite." He enunciated the two terms with exaggerated clarity.

Josef found the trip and the lecture both interesting and agonizing, tormented as he was by his desire to venture further into the caves. Only last night he had announced his plan and its associated queries to the hotel porter: he wanted to descend into the caves as deeply as possible with the area's most experienced cave explorer.

"Then, sir, you want to hire the master painter, Josef Leonhard Betschart. He has been further into Hölloch than anyone else. I'll send the boy immediately," the porter had replied, and at breakfast the following morning he had informed Josef that Betschart sadly would not be available today, but he would be at the gentleman's service early the following morning. He, Betschart, asked the gentleman to appreciate that a trip to the depths of Hölloch would be both a strenuous and a dangerous undertaking that would last a whole day, at least, and possibly two.

Josef sent a message informing Betschart that he would be ready at seven o'clock, rested and dressed in clothing that could withstand soiling. As Josef regarded himself as a man of action, his impatience was now verging on the unbearable.

Andrea drew his attention to a scarlet and rather phallic dripstone. "A stalagmite," she declared gravely with a hint of, or so he thought, vulgar giggling in her voice.

They spent the afternoon strolling in and around Muota. Andrea discovered to her considerable disappointment that the area's only shop was a grocer's, and he sold, in addition to some ugly souvenirs, only items that peasants and mountaineers might want to buy. Nothing for a lady. Josef, however, bought a small hammer. "A geologist's hammer," he enlightened her.

The totality of the darkness took him by surprise. The carbide lamp had run out a couple of kilometers inside the caves, and Josef had never been plunged into such complete darkness. No one can describe it, it has to be experienced, he thought to himself. He didn't say it out loud as Betschart's silence was extremely admonitory. Much time had passed since he last made a noise, let alone uttered a word. Betschart put fresh carbide cubes in the lamp, and they moved on. All around them, chemistry carried out its destructive business: the rain and meltwater, H_2O, absorbed carbon dioxide, CO_2, from the air or the soil thus creating H_2CO_3, which broke down the crystalline structure of the limestone into its basic elements, calcium, Ca^{2+}, magnesium, Mg^{2+}, and carbonate, CO_3^{2-}, which traveled on as ions in the water that formed a stream on the floor of the tunnel. In less than an hour the water flowing past them at this very moment would reach the open waters of the Schlichenden Brunnen River.

To Josef's annoyance, the tunnels went up as often as they went down. His sense of time and direction quickly disappeared beneath the surface of the earth, but even so he realized that they could not have descended very far, and the whole point of the trip was to find the entrance to the world of the Vril-yas. He had asked Betschart when the situation arose to always choose the path leading furthest down, but he had received only a few grunts by way of reply. The intonation had, however, been obliging.

The tunnel they were following mostly by walking, but at times bent double or leopard crawling, was elliptical in shape and had been created from a weaker layer of marl in between the limestone. Once back in the Cretaceous Period, roughly nine geological days ago, a sudden climate change occurred with its associated mass extinction of plants and marine animals. This explains why fossils are frequently found in layers of marl that separate the more homogenous layers of limestone. The clayey layers of marl are softer than the limestone and consequently a natural weak spot—the first to fall victim to the patient ravages of water.

The formation of caves can be divided into four overlapping phases: 1. The initial phase where small channels are eroded into the limestone. 2. The phreatic phase where water flowing under pressure breaks down the limestone and then erodes it by washing it away with sand and stone. 3. The vadose phase where the water level falls and gravity carries away the dissolved limestone. 4. The regolith phase where caves expand as their ceilings collapse. The greatest dangers for a cave explorer are, besides those relating to the technical aspects of mountaineering, rocks falling as a result of regolith and sudden flash floods, known as siphons, which can cut off the route back in no time. November was supposedly the month with the lowest groundwater level, but a sudden rise in the temperature outside could inject colossal amounts of meltwater into the system. Josef glanced at the unimpressive brook on the floor of the tunnel.

Finally they reached a plateau with a steep drop at its edge. Before he started his descent, Betschart hammered a spike into a crack, attached a rope, and indicated, with a look, that Josef should follow. Betschart had taken the lamp, so Josef was left behind alone in the dark. He found the rope and followed suit. As his foot touched the bottom, Betschart suddenly spoke and gave Josef a minor fright.

"This is Tauchstrecke. The deepest part of Hölloch." The guide's leathery face grimaced, and he added, "You need to watch out for flash flooding here."

Josef stamped his boots to get the mud off and said, "There has to be an opening further down."

Betschart said nothing.

"We must look for it," Josef insisted.

The levelheaded Swiss sat down on a rock and took out his pipe. He wasn't paid to run a fool's errand; during their walk to the cave entrance earlier that morning, the Ausburger had told him he was looking for the entrance to an underworld, purportedly inhabited by a superior race, the Vril-something or

other. Betschart didn't care why this man had come
to Hölloch, but he wanted nothing to do with his
esoteric notions. "You look," he said.

Josef took the lamp and started exploring the
chamber. As he moved the beam of light away from
Betschart, the glow from Betschart's pipe seemed to
float in the dark. Josef reached a small lake whose
surface was calm apart from, as he shortly found out,
a small whirlpool at the center. While he fantasized
about where the whirlpool might lead, he started to
notice the silence—or rather its many sounds. Deep
inside the darkness he could hear dripping and
further away, running water. The whirlpool immediately in front of him emitted a high-pitched whis-
tling. Next he became aware of a faint humming,
clearly not produced by the swirling water. The
sound had a ringing, stone-like quality. Josef leapt
up, frightened that a rock was about to dislodge
itself above his head, and he examined the ceiling,
but the humming was constant, which suggested
that no regolith was imminent, and furthermore it
was coming from the darkness. He breathed slowly
and listened out to establish the origin of the sound.
With almost silent footsteps, he followed it until he
found himself facing a large rock sticking out of the
floor of the cave. The rock looked like granite, but

it was a darker type of stone than the surrounding gray limestone. The humming, which had a crunchy undertone, could now clearly be heard. Josef pressed his right ear to the rock, and the sound of almost ten geological days or 125 million years of earthquakes roared against his eardrum.

It was accepted as fact, even in Siedler's time, that earthquakes were the expression of accumulated tension in the Earth's mantle, but the cause was regarded as the planet losing heat and subsequently contracting, whereas today the theory of continental drift, put forward roughly half a geological second later, is generally acknowledged as the explanation for seismic activity.

A small book on geology in the previous century, published in 1923, lists the arguments that cast doubt on the cornerstone of Eduard Suess's theory of contraction and states: "A. Wegener's work, *The Origin of the Alps* (1915), which is rich in interesting opinions, may be regarded as a peculiar consequence thereof. Here the author seeks to explain the formation of mountain ranges and a number of associated phenomena by proposing a theory of reciprocal continental drifts in a horizontal direction. For example, the Atlantic Ocean would have been created by the movements of the American continents away from Europe and Africa; and the American Cordillera were forced up by the resistance which the shift of this western continent encountered." Whereupon the author hastily moves on under the heading: "Surface sculpture, denudation, and sediment formation; and datings derived from them."

Even in those days there was sufficient geological data available to undermine the contraction theory, but it would be another half century before Wegener's continental drift theory won general acceptance. A university textbook claimed as late as 1970:

> "An earthquake is a sudden development of energy within a confined area inside the Earth. The classic explanation (Reid 1911) is that material is stressed due to an increase in tension which at some point exceeds its tensile strength. It is not known what triggers this process."

The same book contains a section on Wegener's continental drift hypothesis.

The canonization of the tectonic plate theory happened in 1972 when the geologist and astronaut Harrison Schmitt from his privileged position onboard *Apollo 17* communicated the following to Mission Control: "I didn't grow up with the idea of drifting continents...but I tell you, when you look at the way the pieces seem to fit together, you could almost make a believer out of anybody."

A parallel and far more prolonged feud between geologists who favored either catastrophism—the theory that the Earth's mantle was shaped by a number of climatic, seismic, et cetera, catastrophes—or actualism—where all geological phenomena are explained through currently active forces as long as these have had enough time in which to be active—had ended in the second half of the nineteenth century with victory going to the latter. "The present is the key to the past" goes a famous quote by Charles Lyell, who in 1830–1833 published his *Principles of Geology* in three volumes and was proclaimed the Father of Geology as evidence to support his theories began to emerge.

Nevertheless, actualism—also known as uniformitarianism—has become the subject of increasing criticism during the twentieth century. Present-day geologists continue to find traces of catastrophes whose consequences register on the geological scale; for example, it's only four thousand years ago, about half a geological minute, that the most recent mega-tsunami, which was over five hundred meters tall and several thousand kilometers wide when it made contact with land, caused the collapse of an island off the west coast of Africa, crossed the Indian Ocean, and laid waste a ten- to twenty-kilometer-wide belt of Southeast Asia and the west-facing coastline of Australia. Predictions indicate that the next mega-tsunami might happen tomorrow or in four thousand years when a chunk of one of the Canary Islands, La Palma, slides into the sea and triggers the destruction of everything on the North, Latin, and South American continents' east-facing coasts. Other catastrophes with geological consequences are meteor strikes and earthquakes, if these are of sufficient magnitude and/or frequency. Earthquakes are divided into three types: volcanic, explosion, and tectonic earth tremors. The first two, however, are very rare, and the millions of quakes that have occurred in the Alpine region, once a very active zone seismically, have virtually all been tectonic. These earthquakes accumulated in the rock massif which the Ausburger, Josef Siedler, pressed his ear against one November day in 1907 and heard a sound that caused him to go deaf in that ear for almost ten minutes.

Shocked, he staggered backwards three steps and clutched his ears because of the sharp pain. Unfortunately, he managed to kick over the lamp in the process, and the carbide holder fell off. Once again the darkness was impenetrable; even the glow of Betschart's pipe was gone. As he fumbled to strike a match, retrieve the various parts of the lamp, and reassemble them, his heart rediscovered a calmer rhythm and the pain subsided. The humming was still audible, but it was nothing compared to what it had been when he pressed his ear against the rock. When the light from the carbide gas had once again banished the darkness, he carefully moved his still functioning left ear to the rock, and the second the delicate cartilage border made contact with it, the force of the roar deprived him of the hearing in that ear, too.

He experienced a silence in his head the likes of which he had never known; even the sound of his heartbeat and the roaring of blood in his ears had gone. But deep within the silence some fragile howling tones slowly grew more distinct. A series of four tones repeated. There was no sudden transition between the tones, but a fast glissando.

Josef sat down on the muddy floor with a bump which he could feel, but not hear. While his ears and their associated neurons struggled to return to their default settings, he sought to memorize the tones reverberating through his head. He tried to sing along even though he could not hear himself. As the howling subsided and his hearing returned, he decided not to tell anyone about the thundering rock. At least not yet. With his geologist's hammer he chipped off a fragment of the rock. An echo ricocheted out into the darkness. Carefully he held up the fragment to his ear; it didn't hum, but he noticed that it quivered very slightly. Mystified, he put it in his pocket.

"About time," was Betschart's only comment when Josef returned soon afterwards.

"I've seen what I wanted," Josef said, and with practically no further conversation they made the long journey out of Hölloch, settled the agreed eight francs, and went their separate ways.

Back at the Hôtel des Grottes, he put the gray and black rock fragment, the size of a walnut, on his bedside table and fell asleep. Andrea returned a little later from a walk in Bödmeren Forest, sat down on the bed, noticed the stone, picked it up, and experienced a peculiar tingling sensation in her fingertips.

On their return to Ausburg, Josef wrote a summary of his experience in Tauchstrecke on a piece of paper which he placed in a small wooden box with the gray and black rock. It was his intention to donate it to the Bavarian State Collection for Paleontology and Geology, but a liquidity crisis in the insurance business and the emotional equivalent in his marriage monopolized his time and thoughts, so the rock and the events associated with it drifted to the twilight of his mind.

Twelve years after their trip to Hölloch, Andrea and Josef were stricken by the Spanish flu like so many others that year, and though both came very close to dying, they did survive. However, when out for a stroll in Provinostraße that same autumn, they had the misfortune that a moving man busy hoisting up a chaise longue to the third floor suffered a coronary just as they walked under the said item of furniture. Andrea was killed instantly, and Josef died from his injuries two days later. The moving man survived.

The marriage had been childless, and it fell to a nephew, a war veteran, to administer the estate. Franz Zweywälder regarded his aunt and uncle as kindhearted and slightly eccentric people, but also as rather bourgeois and detached from reality. During lulls in the war he had undertaken an in-depth study of Peter Kropotkin's *The Conquest of Bread* and Ernst Viktor Zenker's *The Anarchist*, disguised with a cover of Thomas Mann's *Buddenbrooks*. This reading had lit the flame of anarchy in Franz, and he found it a bittersweet delight to sell off the possessions of a deceased bourgeois couple to fund the revolution which at the time, October 1919, had already been suppressed by social democrats loyal to the government in collaboration with the reactionary free corps.

At the end of the war, when Berlin was buzzing with revolutionary zeal, Franz had traveled there with Hans Janssen, a war comrade with the same political views. They shared a flat in Kreuzberg with two other people, Albert Brandt and Hertha Sterbak. It was here that the inaugural meeting of the revolutionary cell ASA (Anti System Action) was held around a wax candle one December night. As they were anarchists, they despised the communists in the Spartacus League.

"They're nothing but state capitalists," Hertha declared. "Property is theft and power is suppression, no matter which form they take."

The communists, for their part, dismissed the anarchists as naïve fantasists, and events in Russia would appear to bear this out: communism was the only feasible alternative to rotten-to-the-core empires and U.S. capitalism.

"But," Albert said, "nothing has really changed: Lenin has turned into a tsar in worker's clothing."

After a discussion lasting a couple of hours, they agreed to carry out direct and sensational but nonviolent actions. They had seen plenty of death already—the men on the battlefield and Hertha at a field hospital. And every day people starved to death in the city's streets.

The group's first action was a triumph: hidden on the roof of 17 Luisenstraße, they emptied latrine buckets and threw horse droppings on Otto Braun, the Prussian minister for agriculture, as he drove past in an open carriage. They also scattered fliers encouraging people to ridicule the authorities rather than allow themselves to be hoodwinked by them; in this the gravest of hours, derisive laughter was the only appropriate response. "The very idea of authority is ridiculous!!!" as the flier proclaimed

with three exclamation marks. They made their get-
away across the roofs, but when they tried to repeat
their success a week later, disaster struck. One of
the soldiers escorting the chief of the war office,
General Wilhelm Groener, whom they had showered
with feces and propaganda moments earlier, shot
Hans with a revolver and hit him in the jaw. Albert
tried to rescue him, but both were caught. Franz
and Hertha escaped only because no one bothered
to look inside an old dovecote where they were hiding. They had made plans to cover this eventuality:
under torture none of them could be expected to
keep quiet. Franz and Hertha left Berlin in opposite directions and didn't tell each other where they
were going.

Franz traveled south to Ausburg where the only
people who knew him were his aunt and uncle,
Andrea and Josef Siedler, two elderly citizens
unlikely to have any contact with the authorities. He
rented an attic room in Senkelbachstraße under the
name Karl Peter Schmidt, and as the months passed
and he grew bored, he started calling at his aunt and
uncle's, mainly to get something to eat. As a result
of the Entente's blockade, Franz experienced, as did
most Germans at the time, the incessant gnawing of
hunger in his stomach.

After the chaise longue accident, Franz, as the only living relative, visited the injured Josef in the hospital, and consequently it was he the undertaker approached when Josef died two days later. The money from the estate paid for the funerals and funded Franz's revolutionary activities—that is to say, it covered his living costs, which enabled him to write. Franz divided up his writing in two genres: lyrical poems and political propaganda. The poetry was in the style of Rainer Maria Rilke's *New Poems*, but it had recently been fruitfully sidelined by Georg Trakl's poems in the magazine *The Arsonist*. In Franz's own opinion, his best poem was a small ode composed during a ten-minute trance of inspiration. On reviewing it, he had made one syntactical change and added an adjective and a line break; otherwise the poem was complete:

> DARK COMES NOVEMBER, DECEMBER
> Winter, deepest of nights, fir trees
>   glisten, hard frost
> Wild singing in the deep frozen traces
>   of autumn.
> Black crows peck on tender hearts,
>   Christmas hearts
> Already entwined in November, you
>   too, unblinking moon,

> Your name is written in ink on icy
>   puddles in the fields.
> Black and restless is the sea, the forests
>   ancient, to the north
> The heron flies mournfully, crying out
> Over the city. And the bells toll
> In the towers; free, without people
> Is this night.

When he emptied the Siedlers' library, he separated the books into two boxes: those he wished to keep and those he intended to sell. The latter made up the majority: Biedermeier novels, travel literature, and numerous volumes on religious and esoteric subjects. There were also a couple of shelves with scientific publications, among which he discovered Kropotkin's *Mutual Aid: A Factor of Evolution*. A consequence of Franz's anarchism and his enormous admiration for the geographer Kropotkin was a favorable disposition towards the natural sciences. Church, state, and capital would be ousted by formal logic and empirical evidence. Another book that ended up in the box of things to keep was Morgenstern's translation of Strindberg's *Black Banners*, whose title compelled him to read it as he sat cross-legged on the floor. He also held on to some art books: Michelangelo, Hieronymus Bosch, Breughel the Elder, Veláquez, and nine volumes of Bong & Co.'s *Library of Golden Classics.*

It took him only two days to dispose of all the goods and chattels which the Siedlers had accumulated during a relatively long life. Everything except the books he was keeping, some clothes, and a small chest of drawers was collected by a furniture dealer, and Franz carted the rest to his attic. The items he kept also included a small wooden box containing a gray-black stone and a short note with the following words: "This is a fragment of rock from Tauchstrecke in Hölloch in Switzerland. It emits a humming sound. I suffered temporarily from deafness after I had listened to the rock. I heard four notes." Franz felt a light tingling in his fingertips when he picked up the stone. The mystery intrigued him, but he had no idea what to do about it, so he put the box in the small chest of drawers with a second note: "This box was found in the estate of Josef and Andrea Siedler, Ausburg, in the year 1919. Signed, Franz Zweywälder."

The chest of drawers would shortly accompany Franz back to Berlin. The only reason for his return was a girl by the name of Judith, the daughter of a bookseller on Askanischer Platz and just seventeen years old. Franz's stomach region had tightened at the sight of this black-haired beauty behind the counter. In the days that followed, he spent hours in the bookshop pretending to flick through books and sneaking, safe behind the bookcases, a peek at the girl. After three days, she had looked up unexpectedly and caught his eye. Bashfully, he looked down, but then he plucked up all his courage and uttered his carefully rehearsed invitation: "May I offer you a glass of orangeade after closing hours?" Her reply followed after an imperceptible pause: "Thank you, but I don't think my father will permit me to." And that had been the end of that. The very thought of asking Moses Brutzkus, the venerable bookseller, had sent Franz fleeing with the doorbell chiming contemptuously after him. The next day the ASA had carried out their fateful action where Hans Janssen got shot in the jaw. Franz's time in Ausburg, however, had not diminished the image of the Jewish girl; on the contrary, he had constructed an entire mythology in her honor.

A year later the aching in his stomach had grown intolerable, and he returned to Berlin despite the risks that that entailed. He grew a pointed beard, shaved his head, and wore his late uncle's clothes supplemented by one or two more recently purchased items in the same conservative style. He took a room at a cheap boarding house in Linkstraße and went straight to the bookshop. He brought with him two letters: one for Judith and one for her father. Both assured them in a few but weighty words of his honorable intentions, accounted—somewhat mendaciously—for his financial circumstances and family situation, and contained the obvious proviso that they had yet to become acquainted and would need an opportunity to do so. In Judith's he had added the following grandiose declaration: "I will love you each and every day as much as the first." He wrote the address of the boarding house at the bottom of his letter to Moses and requested a reply within eight days. The result of this approach was that Moses— who could read between the lines concerning the young suitor's material wealth, knew the status of the boarding house, and furthermore already had a Jewish son-in-law in mind—sought Franz out and ordered him in no uncertain terms to desist.

Meanwhile, his letter had roused Judith's curiosity, and the next day she visited him in secret at the boarding house. Their relationship would never receive society's blessing, but in the time that followed they met repeatedly, both spiritually and carnally. It was in this short period of happiness while they were strolling in the Tiergarten that two plainclothes policemen suddenly seized Franz and took him away. That same morning he had given her the box with the fragment of the humming rock. "You're the Earth's deepest mystery, and this small stone is but a poor tribute. But it's a bit peculiar, don't you think?" he had whispered. For years Judith kept the box to remind her of the bashful young man who was sick with stratospheric love for her.

After Kristallnacht on November 9, 1938, when his bookshop was vandalized, Judith's brother beaten up, and the civil rights of all Jews annulled, Moses finally decided to flee with his family to Denmark, to the city of Aalborg where he had a sister who had offered to take them in. Unfortunately, Judith left her suitcase, which contained the box with the walnut-sized rock, on the train between Hamburg and Flensburg, and her suitcase ended up at the lost property office at Altona Railway Station.

Regulations prescribed that all lost property not claimed after eighteen months became the property of the German Reich Railway, but the official in charge of the office was conscripted when the Second World War broke out on September 1 the following year. He was replaced by a retired ticket clerk, Georg Weide, who guarded the damp wooden hut at the far end of the railway site with its hundreds of suitcases, bags, coats, hats, umbrellas, and so forth, throughout the war, unaware of the regulation. Thanks to a stroke of incredibly good luck and a remote location between two low banks, the hut escaped every single Allied air raid, including the firestorm during Operation Gomorrah on July 28, 1943.

The apartment building in Langenfelder Straße where Georg lived had taken a direct hit as early as May 1941, after which he moved permanently into the hut on the railway site. It turned out to be quite cozy. It already had a stove, a table, a chair, a bed, and an outside lavatory, and he furnished the hut with the few possessions he had managed to dig out from under the rubble. He even hung up a blackout curtain.

It wasn't until December 1943 that Georg finally overcame the inhibitions which had so far deterred him from helping himself to the lost items. He was driven by a noble motive: hunger. One of the suitcases might contain a tin of goulash or a bag of boiled sweets. His approach was systematic: He organized clothing such as coats and hats in neat piles at one end of the hut, making sure that each item retained its original ticket. Then he turned his attention to the suitcases, briefcases, et cetera. One by one he placed them on the table, and feeling like a surgeon with a patient on the operating table, he opened them up and laid out the contents in regimented lines. Then he returned the items in reverse order less anything he needed, which included two fountain pens, a small pile of books, a little money, some clothes, and an antique pocket watch. Whenever he took something, he would replace it with a small note with a brief description of the object and the following sentence: "I, Georg Weide, took this item of lost property at a time of great need." He found very few things that hadn't already rotted, but there was the odd treasure: a packet of sea biscuits and a canvas bag containing ten tins of mackerel, a worn leather holdall with three large bottles of beer and a bottle of plum brandy, and in a hamper he found two large jars of pickled gherkins. He left no notes for the foodstuff. "There's a war on," he said to himself.

During his search he found the box with the fragment of the humming rock. Carefully, he took out the two yellowing notes. His eyes were old and the winter sun barely broke through the dirty window, but by taking his time he managed to read them. He picked up the stone and felt its faint quivering, which frightened him, and he dropped it with a weak falsetto groan. "What sort of fellow are you?" he said into the silence. Judging by the display of objects from the suitcase where he had come across the box with the stone, he took the owner to be a Jewish woman. He picked up the stone from the floor, which caused him some back pain, and assured himself that it really did vibrate. "Wooden box with an unusual stone. I, Georg Weide, took this item of lost property at a time of great need," he wrote on the substitution note for the box, which he pushed under his bed.

Even as a child Georg had been blessed with a remarkable memory combined with a total lack of ambition, and this had led him to a long life of selling train tickets without ever questioning railway fares or procedures. Furthermore, his years behind the ticket window had left him with accurate memories of all the hundreds of thousands of passengers he had served. He spent much of his time in the hut on the railway site ordering this sea of remembered portraits. Initially he organized them according to gender and three age brackets, depending on whether they had requested a child, a standard, or an OAP ticket, and then into three social classes on the basis of first-, second-, or third-class tickets. What other classification principles he should subsequently adhere to became the subject of prolonged deliberation. At first he attempted to sort them according to occupation, but the complications soon multiplied when applying this criterion. For example, was it desirable to distinguish between nannies and wet nurses or between traveling salesmen employed by a firm or working freelance? So many ambiguities arose when he tried to apply economic or social parameters that he was forced to accept that the best basis for archiving people was using features derived only from their faces and not from anything he might deduce from behavior, language, and dress as such conclusions inevitably tended towards prejudice. Ergo, his classification had to observe strictly external factors. He retained the divisions of men, women, children, adults, elderly, first, second, and third class and filed the faces according to length of noses, which after a couple of indeterminate cases he redefined to nose volume.

He patiently sorted his memory up to one day in September 1944 where the work was irrefutably complete. The final archive contained 361,412 people exactly. Strangely breathless, he considered it with his mind's eye. In the days that followed, he experienced a profound sense of emptiness. He tried to return to the archive and invented questions such as "the number of noses with three or more anomalies, warts, abundant hair growth, et cetera," or "the greenest eyes," but how could he define "anomaly," "abundant," or "green" without wading straight into the quicksand of subjectivity? The futility of the entire enterprise mocked him, and several days passed where he would not even think about the archive.

Anyway, searching for food and fuel took up plenty of time. He looked through every item of lost property again and took anything he could sell on the black market. Every time he left a note. I've written this sentence five hundred times now, he thought one day, having dotted the full stop after "a time of great need" on a note that replaced a pair of leather gloves.

One day in December a small, emaciated boy appeared at the hut. Georg had just returned from town with the catch of the day, which had been good, a jar of salted herring and a crust of pumpernickel bread, when he heard a light cough coming from inside the hut. He tiptoed closer and surprised the boy in the act of rummaging through his belongings. The boy was barely ten years old, his clothes were rags, and his blond hair a matted cake of blood and mud.

"Hey, you!" Georg exclaimed, and the startled boy tried to escape, but Georg blocked the door with his seventy-nine-year-old body. The boy darted across to the opposite corner of the hut and watched him with anxious and aggressive eyes. Georg closed the door behind him with an "Ah, well," and unpacked his food. He took some of the bread, a herring, and a mug of rainwater colored only slightly gray from the constant smoke in the air and pushed it towards the boy, who, when he finally dared to come forward, wolfed down the food in seconds. "Such hunger," Georg remarked. He introduced himself and asked for the boy's name, but he got no reply. "You can stay here if you haven't got anywhere to go," he added. The boy didn't reply, but he made himself a bed out of two suitcases and covered himself with a winter coat. Georg lit a fire in the stove.

The boy, whose name was Ferdinand Höffel, stayed with Georg in the hut for the rest of the war. His entire family had been wiped out. His parents had been arrested by the Gestapo even before the war started, and the four children under the leadership of the two eldest, Jürgen, known as Jöggi, and Beate, fifteen and thirteen years old at the time, had

had to fend for themselves. The air raids had killed all his siblings.

Georg and Ferdinand formed a close bond. The old man had never had a wife or children and decided that this was his last chance of anyone remembering him after his undoubtedly imminent death. The boy had nothing but a voracious hunger and a similar need for safety.

Georg taught Ferdinand to read, write, and do simple arithmetic. He remembered some of what he had himself been taught, though it was a long time ago. There were a few schoolbooks among the lost property, but Georg had never liked the bombastic rhetoric of the Nazis and preferred to use a copy of Ernst Wiechert's *The Simple Life* from 1939 as his textbook. This novel, of which more than 250,000 copies had been sold despite the animosity of the Nazis, was an expression of what would later be termed "inner emigration." After the diaspora of the brain which followed Hitler's assumption of power in 1933 and the subsequent blatant suppression of every kind of dissent by the "spiritual revolution" of the Nazis, many Germans chose to seek refuge in apolitical and eternal spheres and keep their souls untainted, if nothing else. They switched off the radio and read Goethe, Schiller, Hamsun's *Growth of the Soil*, or Ernst Wiechert's novel about Thomas von Orla, a naval captain from the recently ended First World War who, disillusioned by the realization of the futility of his middle-aged life, abandons his family in town "to start over." His leaving is triggered by Psalm 90:9: "We spend our years as a tale that is told." He settles down on a wooded island in one of the Masurian lakes in East Prussia and finds peace and insight alone in nature. The author of this novel had recently returned from internment in Buchenwald, an experience he described in *The Forest of the Dead*, written in 1939 and published in 1945. Writing *The Simple Life* was to Wiechert "the sanctuary, the invulnerable, the inviolable, where you can escape the world of the loudspeaker, the marches, the informers, the barbed wire." His tiny, invulnerable kingdom was re-created in the hut on the railway site as Ferdinand spelled his way through the story of Thomas von Orla, whose only wish was to be "like a stone on the ground." "No adventures, no heroics, no laurels on my brow. Set my nets and drag them, keep the house and the island clean, read a few pages and sit by the water in the evening and gaze at the stars."

"I've never seen a lake in a forest," Ferdinand said one day.

"The war will be over soon," Georg replied. "Then we'll go to Fleesensee. It's a lake in the east; I went there on a school camping trip many years ago. It's nice. We can go fishing."

From then on the two of them discussed at length what they would do when the war ended. They intended to leave the town and build a cabin in the forest. Georg would fish and grow vegetables, and Ferdinand would look for work, possibly as a woodcutter or gamekeeper so they would have money for tobacco, sugar, et cetera. They would live peacefully and follow the rhythms of the day and the seasons. They would have a dog and keep chickens, possibly a cow too. "Do you remember butter?" Georg asked.

One day he showed Ferdinand the small, inexplicably quivering stone. "That Tauchstrecke in Hölloch in Switzerland must be a cave of some sort. Look," Georg said, pointing to the stone's flat side, "marks from a chisel or a hammer. This piece was chipped off a larger rock. The note says it hums."

"One day I'll travel to Switzerland and solve the mystery," Ferdinand promised.

From Georg's dictation he wrote a third note and enclosed it with the stone: "Found in 1943 in the lost property office of the German Reich Railway,

Hamburg-Altona line. Signed, Georg Weide and
Ferdinand Höffel."

At the start of May, the British arrived and
brought their peace. A month later the old man
and the boy broke out and walked eastwards with a
hand truck piled high with bursting suitcases until
they reached Fleesensee. Before they left the hut,
Ferdinand persuaded George to relax his misplaced
loyalty towards a railway company which now barely
existed and distribute the lost property among the
people in the town.

"The clothes lie in moth-eaten piles while people
freeze to death in the street at night."

They helped themselves to everything they
needed and gave away the rest one morning on
Kaiserplatz. Ferdinand shuttled between the hut and
the town square with the hand truck. Georg watched
the hollow faces flocking around him. Then they
set off on the long road to Fleesensee. They walked
slowly; Georg was eighty, after all, so it took them
more than three weeks, but the weather was mostly
fair, and when humming filled the skies, it was only
transport planes and not bombers.

Twice they saw cheering British soldiers circling
one of their mates who was raping a woman. The
first time Georg placed a hand over Ferdinand's

eyes, but the boy removed it, saying, "I've seen that before." His sister, Beate, had been forced to sell her only valuable possession to black marketers many times. This was before a shell fragment tore open her neck.

"It's the victor's spoils," Georg said. "It has been this way since the time of Alexander. Even so, the world has never seen a war like this. Then again, that's what they said about the last one. At least the Brits only do it when their officers aren't looking."

People coming from the East told lurid stories about the behavior of the Soviet soldiers. Georg and Ferdinand never met any Russians themselves until they were on the other side of Schwerinersee, but fortunately they weren't interested in an old man and a boy.

Once they arrived at Malchow, they followed the shore until they reached a tongue of land between Fleesensee, Kölpinsee, and Jabelscher See. Some distance into the forest they came across an abandoned log cabin. It had been empty for a long time; the windows were smashed, there were holes in the roof, and mouse and bird droppings were everywhere, but to their eyes it was perfection. It was in this small cabin, leaning up against its wooden walls and staring into its stone-built fireplace, that Ferdinand would live out the most part of his life. They began renovating the house, and the work progressed in an almost playful atmosphere until Georg fell ill the fourth day and died the same night.

"Old age, exhaustion, hunger, happiness—any one of them can kill you," he said. Ferdinand dug a grave near an oak and struggled to get the shrouded body into it.

Ferdinand was only eleven years old, but he had seen enough drama to last him a lifetime and was determined to create a safe routine for himself in the cabin. He picked mushrooms, berries, beechnuts, and chestnuts. He hunted hares and pheasant with a bow and flint-headed arrows. He set traps and caught a fawn and a couple of foxes. For a while he ate hedgehogs, which he covered in clay and baked on the embers. When he cracked open the sooty lumps, hedgehog spines and fur would stick to the clay shells. In order not to be discovered, he only lit fires after sunset. He blacked out the windows for the same reason. He built a lookout high up in a pine from where he could survey the whole area. He organized his days into practical tasks that were both numerous and eminently sensible. Questioning the reason for collecting rainwater was pointless.

The silence and the solitude comforted his soul. He took great care never to be seen by anyone; if he as much as heard voices or dogs barking, he would disappear deeper into the shadows. He wanted nothing to do with people; they would either kill him or abandon him by dying. Ferdinand's isolation caused him to construct an inner monologue where he referred to himself as Cousin Fox. "As long as Cousin Fox is here, then death isn't," he would mutter, unaware that he was echoing the Epicureans. "And when it comes, then he no longer is. As long as Cousin Fox is alone, he need not fear death."

One moonless night three years after his arrival at the cabin, however, his curiosity got the better of him. He ventured as far as the village of Jabel, where he stole a ham, but an old woman saw him run away, and she told her husband, who mentioned it to his chess partner, who passed it on to his daughter, who informed her husband, who was the secretary of the Waren branch of the newly formed Socialist Unity Party of Germany, and he, keen to be useful, alerted the children's welfare office in Neustrelitz that a "feral child" had been seen in Jabel. Nine men came looking for the boy and caught him after their dogs had chased him up a tree. It wasn't unusual in wartime Germany for orphans to flee to the forest, but they tended to appear of their own accord or had been found soon after the capitulation. Ferdinand's success in hiding for so long resulted in a paragraph in the newspaper, *Neues Deutschland*:

> FERAL CHILD FOUND IN FOREST
> —Neustrelitz, Soviet Occupation Zone, September 9, 1948
> The famous story of Kaspar Hauser has repeated itself the heart of the anti-fascist zone. A boy who has been hiding in the forest between Malchow and Waren since the end of the war has been found and taken to the orphanage, Free Beginning, in Neustrelitz. The poor child has regressed to a feral stage during his long isolation in the forest. Even so he will learn to enjoy the fruits of solidarity. The principal of the orphanage, Comrade Ernst Joachim Schemmler, says, "The bad days are over for this boy."

At the orphanage Ferdinand got the bottom bunk bed, a Free German Youth uniform, and one meal a day, almost invariably potatoes or rutabagas. From the first day the one year older Jürgen Eberhard, known as Jöggi, took him under his wing. Ferdinand had vowed never to become attached to another human being again and was also spooked by the coincidence of his protector sharing his name with his late brother, but eventually he dropped his guard and devoted himself to the friendship.

Together, Jöggi and Ferdinand distanced themselves from a world where absurdity and anxiety were recurrent themes. They smoked stolen cigarettes and performed biting parodies of the apparatchiks' vacuous permutations of rhetorical concepts such as "socialism," "fatherland," and "solidarity."

"They've infested those words like worms, sucked out their true meaning and left only empty shells," Jöggi declared. "Besides, their militaristic aesthetics betray them: Free German Youth is Hitler Youth all over again. Or consider the irony that we're captives in an institution with the word 'free' in its name."

Ferdinand nodded in agreement in between blowing distorted smoke rings.

The children at the orphanage went to school and worked on rebuilding the town for nine hours every day. In practice what this meant was that every morning they marched in brigade formation to a reclaiming facility where they searched for useable materials, knocked mortar off bricks, straightened out pipes, and so on while listening to the brigade leader reading aloud edifying texts through a scratchy loud-speaker or singing hymns to communism. Ferdinand could never understand why he always felt sad when they sang the second verse of "The Internationale."

> No savior from on high delivers.
> No trust we have in prince or peer.
> Our own right hand the chains must
>   shiver.
> Chains of hatred, greed, and fear.
> Ere the thieves will out with their
>   booty
> And to all give a happier lot.
> Each at his forge must do his duty
> And strike the iron while it's hot.

One summer day they escaped temporarily from the orphanage and visited the cabin, which fortunately, as it turned out, the authorities had yet to discover. Their intention wasn't to stay there—people would start looking for and ultimately find them—but to seal the cabin and hide Ferdinand's belongings, which in addition to clothes, suitcases, tools, and a couple of books included a box with a quivering stone the size of a walnut.

"The humming stone," Ferdinand called it with reference to one of the notes in its box.

"One day we'll go to Switzerland to solve the mystery," Jöggi declared.

"Yes, I made that promise once," Ferdinand said.

They broke up some floorboards and dug out a pit where they hid his things. Afterwards they returned the floorboards and covered up any evidence of disturbance. They also planted willow twigs around the cabin. "When we're sixteen and get out, we'll meet up here," they promised each other.

Their time at Free Beginning never tamed the rebellious Jöggi; Ferdinand, on the other hand, slowly began to conform.

"If it's peace and quiet I'm craving," he reasoned to himself, "it's important not to draw attention to myself, toe the line. Do what they expect of me."

Little by little he began navigating through the community by reviving his old dream of becoming a gamekeeper or a forester.

As Jöggi's sixteenth birthday approached, he started talking about the West Zone.

"But we're going to live in the cabin," objected Ferdinand, who had another year left before he regained his freedom, or its interpretation as practiced in the Soviet Occupation Zone.

"No, pal, the future lies to the west. Over there you can put your trust in the only person you can really rely on: yourself," Jöggi replied. "Soon the border will close for good. The communists over here are nuts."

Ferdinand didn't disagree with these views, but they mattered less when he thought about the cabin in the forest—the cabin and the forest where he had experienced the only happiness in his life.

"I'm staying here, in the forest." He recognized the feeling of betrayal.

"I'll visit you if I can," Jöggi said.

The previous evening they had spoken about the humming stone.

"It'll be easier for you to travel to Switzerland," Ferdinand had said. "So you should take the stone. Come back or write me a letter and tell me what you find down there in Hölloch."

Jöggi promised to do so and stopped at the cabin before he headed for Hamburg, taking the small box in his rucksack.

Ferdinand realized his dream of a quiet life in the cabin on the headland between Fleesensee, Kölpinsee, and Jabelscher See. Officially, he lived in a block of flats in Malchow, but as he was a party member at activist level, the authorities overlooked his neglect of solidarity duties locally and left him alone in the cabin where months would pass without him seeing anyone. His organization of daily tasks reached a level which, in his own opinion, bordered on perfection. There wasn't a single wasted minute in his day.

He never heard from Jöggi. After the fall of the Berlin Wall, he obtained the telephone numbers of thirty-seven different Jürgen Eberhards in the Federal Republic of Germany, but he never summoned up the courage to call. He would have liked to travel to the West, possibly even to Switzerland.

"But Cousin Fox has grown too old to travel," he said to himself.

Jöggi reached Hamburg on September 19, 1949, two days before the federal government assumed the role of the Allied forces. The wind was strong but not cold, and he was utterly exhausted but proud of his achievement after his four-day march.

"I survived," he whispered to himself when he reached Zeughausmarkt and took in the re-emerging city. The traces of the war were ever present, but here and there new facades rose from the ruins, carts laden with boxes crossed the square, and women cultivated little vegetable gardens in between the rubble. There wasn't one of them who hadn't lost several loved ones, and yet their laughter rang out in the wind. Time had passed and would forever do nothing but that: Go. Forwards.

Jöggi didn't want to look back either. A couple of days later he continued southbound, this time on the roof of a truck until he reached Düsseldorf, where he rented an attic room in Oberblik, found work as a clerk at a steel rolling mill, and started saving up though he hadn't yet decided what for. He enjoyed watching the figures grow in his savings book. Money equals freedom, he thought.

On his days off, he explored the city. One April morning he sat cracking hazelnuts on a collapsed wall by the Rhine when he spotted a young woman drawing what he assumed to be his portrait, judging from her frequent glances in his direction. He strolled over to her with a confident swagger, but one look at her sketchpad told him he had been mistaken: the drawing was a mishmash of small squares in shades of gray and black with a single blood red dot. At first he thought it wasn't supposed to resemble anything specific, but slowly buildings and figures started to emerge from the chaos. Everything in the drawing was in motion.

It wasn't until then that he looked at her. She was dark-haired and beautiful, but he had noticed that even from a distance. Now he discovered that she was slightly cross-eyed. She didn't look back at him, nor did she ignore him.

"It makes you dizzy. It looks like an earthquake."

"It's simply viewed differently. Look, that's you," she said, indicating a collision of three gray squares in one corner.

"Who are you?" he asked.

"My name's Marianne Hecht. I'm going to be an artist."

"I'm Jöggi. I'm going to be a capitalist."

"That's death," she said, pointing to the red dot.

Jöggi and Marianne became an item. She drew and painted; he worked his way up the hierarchy at the steel rolling mill. The years passed. In 1956 Jöggi started his first business, a small art supplies shop at the corner of Klosterstraße and Kurfürstenstraße called Eberhard Art Supplies. The fact that Marianne was an extrovert and socially skilled person who knew practically everyone on the Düsseldorf art scene contributed considerably to the shop's success. As the years went by, Jöggi's enterprise grew to include a wholesale business, and in 1960 when Marianne accepted a place at the Academy of Fine Arts in Düsseldorf, Jöggi put a trusted employee in charge of the shop and went into the gallery and art dealer business where the real money was to be made. He was especially lucky acquiring and selling two Otto Dix paintings, twelve Francis Picabia drawings, and later, three monochromes by Yves Klein. Jöggi's gallery was called Gallerie E and was located in Hunsrückestraße. His office was on the first floor where he sat in state behind a wide desk, permitted himself to be addressed as "Herr Direktor," and offered any guests who smoked a light from a silver table lighter set in a marble block.

Jöggi's appreciation of visual art as primarily a product in a capitalist system and only secondarily as a cultural expression derived from Marianne, who happily aired this cynical view during numerous discussions at the academy. She studied with Professor Joseph Fassbender, but traveled independently to London where she saw the exhibition "This Is Tomorrow" in Whitechapel Art Gallery, which proved to be a turning point in her career. Her thinking and the works created as a result owed much to the ideas of Yves Klein, who sometimes lectured at the academy. Joseph Beuys, whom Marianne on her first encounter had categorized as a pompous fool, was a negative influence. Marianne mentioned one of her heroes, Marcel Duchamp, and Beuys had made a face and snarled, "Duchamp was once the starting point for something he couldn't possibly have fore-seen, but now he's little more than a chess player and an escapist." Whereupon he made it clear with a dis-missive gesture that the topic was exhausted. Later in discussions with Beuys's ever-growing number of disciples, she consistently referred to him as "Papa Prophet."

After graduating from the academy in 1964, Marianne held her first solo exhibition in Jean-Pierre Wilhelm's Galerie 22 in Kaiserstraße. At the heart of the exhibition was a series of lithographs, *Anti Object I-XII*, which depicted a series of random objects in non-realistic proportions: forks, screws, shoes, spectacles, walking sticks, typewriters, tooth-brushes, and so on. There were also two sculptures, a kind of objets trouvés: two fish tanks filled with soiled linen from the maternity ward of St. Martinus Hospital and withered flowers from Eller Cemetery. The acquisition of both the flowers and the linen had involved criminality on her behalf which went undetected—regrettably, in Marianne's opinion. She had been looking forward to telling a judge that

the thefts had been an artistic act, but turning herself in at the police station or going to the press felt
like a vulgar betrayal of her actions.

The final object in her exhibition was entitled *Central
European Mystery*. It was the wooden box with the humming stone, which Marianne had sealed with yellow
plastic tape. The three notes inside the box were now
accompanied by a fourth which stated that "Marianne
Hecht wrote this note in 1964 in Düsseldorf. I hereby
declare this box—and its contents—to be art." She had
been given the box by Jöggi, who was well aware that
by so doing he was breaking his promise to Ferdinand,
and as a result he made her draw up a contract to be
signed by a potential buyer of the work. The buyer
would be obliged to travel to the location mentioned in
the document inside the box and seek to solve the mystery of its contents. According Marianne's wishes, the
removal of the plastic tape must only be undertaken as
an "artistically defensible action." Three copies of the
contract were produced: one for the seller, one for the
buyer, and a spare to copy in case the work was sold
on. The contracts were exhibited on the same plinth
as the box.

The exhibition poster listed her name at the top
and the title, *Useful/Useless*, and below there was a
reproduction of *Anti Object I*, which contained part of

a sofa cushion, an Anglepoise lamp, a soup tureen, and a carburetor. At the very bottom the following hermetic sentence could be seen: "The screw tightens the thread of the past. Whoosh!"

Judging by Marianne's own free market principles, the exhibition was a success since the owner of Remscheid Scrap Merchants, Johannes Pedrag Irmnitz-Bismarck and his wife, Patricia, bought all twelve lithographs and *Central European Mystery*. Johannes Pedrag was born in 1928 and old enough to join the army when the last conscription orders were issued in 1945, but during his brief military training he suffered an accidental explosion which scarred his face and destroyed the sight in his right eye, and he was never sent to the front. After the war he completed his business college education and started, with the help of a dramatically reduced family fortune, the scrap yard in Remscheid. Pedra, as his wife called him, was a soft-spoken man, a creature of habit, a conscientious manager of his small business as well as a passionate collector of contemporary visual art, an interest he shared with his wife Patricia, née Bauer, and known as Patti.

It was pure chance that they didn't collect butterflies or operetta scores. It had come about because Patti's uncle, who died in 1957 after a life as a sculptor sculpting mostly busts of citizens in Cologne and Remscheid, had lectured his family on his deathbed with a trembling index finger and breaking voice that art was the jewel in the crown of civilization and by promoting art its natural ideals, truth and beauty, would spread into every corner of society like ripples in the water. "Protect art. It's the antidote to the innate barbarism of the human race."

Pedra and Patti became collectors of the latest visual art, and as they visited local galleries and museums, read various leaflets, and spoke to several artists and art dealers, they formed their own opinion on the subject. They were especially influenced by their meeting and subsequent friendly association with Norbert Kricke, sculptor and from 1964 professor at the Academy of Fine Arts in Düsseldorf.

Marianne Hecht's *Central European Mystery* went straight to the heart of their concept of genuine modern art. "This box cuts across several disciplines," Patti exclaimed. "This work is about art versus non-art, about secrecy and curiosity. It sneers at the bureaucratic society, and in particular, it

questions the relationship between the artist and the
buyer! The artistic effort is hidden from our non-
artistic eyes. The restored, true, artistic Utopia is
inside this box! We have to have that work, Pedra."
As Pedra only rarely disagreed with Patti and he too
was intrigued by the box with the plastic tape, he
replied, "We'll take it, sweetie."

In the time that followed they toyed with the idea
of breaking the seal on the box, but refrained. This
niggling curiosity was precisely the artist's intention,
and besides, they had signed a contract agreeing not
to do so unless it happened as an "artistically defensible action," something they didn't feel capable of
undertaking, let alone able to articulate what that
meant. Consequently, the box remained unopened
on a shelf in their villa in Remscheid.

In the summer of 1981, Herr and Frau Irmnitz-
Bismarck celebrated their silver wedding anniver-
sary by vacationing in Fuengirola on the Costa del
Sol in Spain where they happened to meet Marianne
Hecht. They had briefly been introduced back in
1964, and Patti instantly recognized the woman in
the wide-brimmed hat who was idly turning a post-
card display stand.

"Excuse me, you're Marianne Hecht, aren't you?"
was Patti's opening line.

Marianne was startled, but she quickly composed herself and replied, "Yes, and you're...you bought some lithographs once..."

"That's right. Patricia Irmnitz. What a pleasure. And this is my husband, Pedra."

Handshakes were exchanged, less enthusiastically on Marianne's side, but she accepted the offer of a cup of coffee at a nearby sidewalk restaurant and the accompanying friendly cross-examination: Yes, she lived here permanently now, in a house, ten kilometers inland. No, she no longer practiced art. Well, because she had discovered that advertising, for example, had a greater impact, and since learning that there were more important things in life, to begin with she had had children. Thank you. Two boys; they would be back from school soon. They exchanged some more general information and commented on the coffee and the heat until Marianne said goodbye and left. The *Central European Mystery* was never mentioned, something which later irked Patti a little.

Eight years later Pedra died suddenly from lung failure. Two months later Patti decided that loneliness was worse than death, took three sleeping pills, went to the garage, put the key in the ignition, and died very quietly.

The will left the Irmnitz-Bismarck Collection to the Nordrhein-Westfalen Museum of Art in Düsseldorf in place of death duties, which based on the most recent valuation from the insurance company must be regarded as very reasonable. A statement from the museum showed that the collection consisted of 187 items in total, of which the most valuable were five drawings by Joseph Beuys and two Gerhard Richter paintings. The statement was prepared by the East Berlin born and raised art historian Ulrike Breslauer. She had lived in Düsseldorf since 1986 when she was granted permission to leave East Germany. She got a job at the museum, which had recently moved to the black, curved block on Grabbeplatz and was looking for staff to register the artifacts that would occupy all the new galleries. This building, designed by Dissing & Weitling of Copenhagen and mentioned in hushed tones by local politicians and architectural writers, was an object of decided hatred on Ulrike's part. It reminded her of the concrete brutalism of East Germany, only with five times the budget and ten times the need for prestige—the same vast, uniform surfaces that spurned nature's small individuals who would be using the building.

Ulrike lived alone, which was unintentional, but finding a man who suited her and vice versa seemed an insurmountable task. At the same time, she cherished her little eccentricities. For example, she might live for months on pancakes which she ate standing as she cooked them, she breathed noisily when she did yoga, and she went to the bathroom with the door open, all the lights off, and Hendrix thumping on the stereo. Such actions were impossible in East Berlin, where she had inadvertently married a man who proved to be a jealous and petty wimp. With each year the marriage had become increasingly intolerable, so when fate offered her the chance to travel to the West, she didn't hesitate. Her parents had died, and her only close relative in East Germany was a brother she rarely spoke to.

As she never watched television or read the newspapers, the late summer events of 1989 where tens of thousands of East Germans marched, scaled the fences of the Western embassies in Budapest, Prague, and Warsaw, and traveled to Western Europe via Hungary escaped Ulrike's attention. One day in the canteen when a colleague solicited her opinion on the "dramatic events on the other side," Ulrike's face displayed a look of incomprehension, and after the dumbfounded question, "But don't you care even a little?" she had things explained to her. "And," the explanation concluded, "the question now is whether the East German government will deploy the army. They stand alone; it doesn't look like the Soviets will send in their tanks this time. Three years ago Gorbachev launched the Sinatra Doctrine, which allows East European countries to choose their own way without interference."

"Aha," Ulrike had said. "Who's Gorbachev?"

Her colleague's jaw dropped. "What planet have you been living on these past four years?"

In the time that followed, Ulrike took more of an interest in the media, which could barely keep up with events, and finally as autumn turned to winter, her own opinion took shape: it might be acceptable that West Germany swallowed up East Germany, and indeed it looked likely that this would happen since the only real power is financial, but it would be preferable if Germany could find her own way between capitalism and socialism. This opportunity would, however, be missed just like in 1952 when the Soviet Union had proposed a united, demilitarized, and alliance-free Germany. Never mind, she thought. On November 9 Ulrike considered traveling to Berlin, but she decided to wait until the Christmas holidays. She had a job to do.

Her work on the Irmnitz-Bismarck Collection progressed steadily until one day she sat with Marianne
Hecht's small box in front of her. The contents might
require conservation, was one justification for her
urge to succumb to her curiosity. Whether a given
action is art is a question of definition, was another.
"Every human being is an artist," she quoted Joseph
Beuys and cut the yellow plastic tape with a scalpel.
Her excuse proved to be valid: the small notes inside
were badly ravaged by time, and it wasn't until she
put them under a microscope that she was able to
read them. Afterwards she prepared the following
descriptive inventory for the museum's archive:

> S-14/32 HECHT, Marianne (1928–
> 1987). *Central European Mystery.* 1964.
> Cherry wood. Paper. Stone. Plastic.
>
> The work consists of a wooden box
> (measuring 7.6 × 5.8 × 3.1 cm), sealed
> with 4 cm wide yellow plastic tape,
> and two copies of a contract. The con-
> tract states that the tape may only be
> removed in an "artistically defensible"
> manner and includes the condition
> that the buyer must seek to solve "the
> mystery hidden within the box." The

contract between the buyer (Patricia Irmnitz-Bismarck) and the seller (the artist) was concluded on October 12, 1964. The second copy of the contract is blank, and the following sentence has been added to its title: "To be copied in case the work is sold on to a new buyer."

The wooden box contains a small, gray-black stone (max. diameter 3.4 cm) and four handwritten notes as follows:

"This is a rock fragment from Tauchstrecke in Hölloch in Switzerland. It emitted a humming sound. I suffered temporarily from deafness after I had listened to the rock. I heard four notes." (Item 1)

"This box was found in the estate of Josef and Andrea Siedler, Ausburg, in the year 1919. Signed, Franz Zweywälder." (Item 2)

"Found in 1943 in the lost property office of the German Reich Railway,

Hamburg-Altona line. Signed, Georg
Weide and Ferdinand Höffel." (Item 3)

"Marianne Hecht wrote this note in
1964 in Düsseldorf. I hereby declare
this box—and its contents—to be art."
(Item 4)

As she proceeded to catalogue the remaining items,
her thoughts kept returning to the quivering stone.
We really ought to copy the blank contract, she
thought, and fill in the museum's details. The work
had in effect been sold on, and the obligation speci-
fied in the contract had to be assigned to someone.
Without informing the museum's management—
she judged the matter to be too trifling—she photo-
copied the contract, contacted the solicitor who had
acted as the administrator of the Irmnitz-Bismark
estate, and asked him to act as the seller, after which
she signed as the buyer on behalf of the Nordrhein-
Westfalen Museum of Art. It was now the museum's
responsibility, but in practice her task to attempt to
solve the riddle of the stone.

First she had to establish the nature of the
mineral, so she took the stone for analysis at the
Department of Geology in the Institute of Geography

at the Heinrich Heine University, where a geologist by the name of Frank Kaufmann explained that the stone was a chip of amphibolite, also known as hornblende slate. This crystalline slate was formed by high metamorphose degrees of either marl rock or basal rock and was common in bedrock areas. He measured the faint quivering to a frequency of 130 hertz with an amplitude of 2.1 micrometers, but he could not provide a satisfactory explanation of the phenomenon.

"It's truly mysterious," he said to Ulrike. "Perhaps someone should find out where this fragment comes from."

"Venturing down into Hölloch?"

"It would appear so."

In this period Ulrike's thoughts turned increasingly to Hecht's *Central European Mystery*. She read extracts of library books on geology, mineralogy, and the formation of mountains and caves. Researching the names of the individuals mentioned in the notes produced nothing; many archives had been lost during the war, and the names might be fictional, though an analysis of the paper showed that they had most probably been written at the time they claimed to be, and they were clearly not in Hecht's handwriting. Ulrike studied the history of Hölloch and spoke on the telephone to the retired geomorphologist Alfred Bögli, who in his capacity as an authority on Hölloch stated that no one knew anything about a humming rock in Tauchstrecke, but he also conceded that the number of visitors was limited since Tauchstrecke was frequently flooded.

In the meantime, East Germany had imploded, and the territory and its 16 million inhabitants were incorporated into West Germany. West German campaign money had funded East Germany's first "free" election, and Helmut Kohl was made chancellor of the "reunited" Germany. Ulrike always marked these words with air quotes when she said them, but in truth she feigned more outrage than she genuinely felt; the peaceful East German revolution was now history, and even capitalism's freedom to be poor and lonely was preferable to the open prison of state socialism. Resignation was an obvious response for her, she thought, born into a nation with a tradition of backdoor revolutions. Her train of thought contemplated the peculiar German phenomenon, the stab-in-the-back legend, and interpreted it as the treachery of the rear guard or more generally as further evidence of how the impulsive extinction under the influence of external forces thrived in numerous forms, right down to individuals.

An interesting artist such as Marianne Hecht would appear to have felt betrayed and underrated, or at least that was what Ulrike read between the lines in the short biography of her in Ulrika Evers's *German Women Artists in the Twentieth Century* and in a short essay entitled "What Now for Art?" in the magazine *Prospect* in 1967 where Hecht wrote, "We should not delude ourselves by thinking that art has a chance of reaching ordinary people as well. If something is true beyond the narrow circle, it is inevitably in a diluted, if not perverted form." At the end of the 1960s, Hecht had stopped producing visual art and started working as a graphic designer with an advertising agency. In 1987 she died in a swimming pool accident in southern Spain. Perhaps there's no such thing as an ordinary person, Ulrike thought to herself.

After being haunted by the *Central European Mystery* for a year, Ulrike contacted the geologist Frank Kaufmann again to ask if he would come with her to Switzerland. "Hölloch?" Frank, too, had been pondering the stone whose quivering could not be explained by any available model, but he had shelved the question for career reasons. If he presented this enigma to a scientific forum, the result would either be ridicule or a silence that would speak volumes. Besides, his wife had just given birth to their second child.

"Come back and tell me what you find. I'll get you a DAT recorder and a one hundred hertz vibra-meter to take down into the caves. If there really is a rock which hums or quivers, we need to document it."

So Ulrike set off alone. At Mannheim she started to cry, and she didn't stop until she reached Freiburg. The reason for her emotional outburst wasn't solely the humming stone, but also the geologist, Frank, who had likewise been on her mind in the preceding twelve months, but shyness and self-loathing had prevented her from doing anything about it, and it wasn't until his casual remark about his wife and their second child that she realized how utterly unattainable her dreams were. Over a cup of black coffee at a petrol station before the border she started to redefine her life. "No more vacillation and cowardice," she wrote on a paper napkin. "No more leaving all decisions to inertia. No more waiting for fate. From now on I'll follow my impulses. No more self-deception."

That evening she reached Zurich and found a cheap hotel where she showered, put on makeup—a rare event for her—and went out into the city. She thought the world would reveal its uncharted regions to her reopened eyes, but all she found in the Swiss night was repetition: the bartender who reigned in his mini kingdom in an underpaid service sector, the smell of sour beer from the mouth of a lonely idiot, and the cold wind that followed her home. She had to try a different approach. Denying the past wasn't the way forward since that also involved being stuck in something other than the present. "I'm here," she said out into the empty hotel room as she tapped her ribcage with her index finger.

The next morning she drove to Hölloch. Before her departure she had booked a place on a two-day guided tour with the Outdoor Adventure Trekking Team. Eight hours after leaving the surface, they stopped for a break at Bivouac 1, and it wasn't until then that she discovered that not only had the guide no intention of taking the four participants down into Tauchstrecke, but he could also not be persuaded to do so.

"Too dangerous," he insisted. "For safety reasons we must keep to established routes. There might be someone from the Hölloch Cave Research

Association who can be talked into taking you down there. But you won't be covered by insurance as you are now."

Ulrike had to accept this and stay with the group for the rest of the trip, but back at the hotel thirty-six hours later she made up her mind and drove to Schwyz where she bought mountaineering equipment in order to venture deep into Hölloch on her own. Anything for art, she thought, and entered her PIN code.

The contractual obligation to attempt to solve the mystery of the humming stone was the ideal hook on which Ulrike could hang her actions. It was real and happening right now. After a short sleep she rose at one o'clock in the morning and waded through virgin snow to the entrance of the cave. She checked her equipment by moonlight one last time and put the first cartridge in the carbide lamp. Her entire being felt purposeful and energetic.

It took her twenty-three hours to trek the nearly three kilometers to the place where the map indicated that Tauchstrecke opened out from the bottom of the black shaft where the tunnel ended. She found the by now rusty peg which Josef Leonhard Betschart had hammered into the rock eighty-three years ago, attached a rope, and lowered herself down.

After a few minutes in the large tunnel she heard the constant humming. Stepping quickly through the water which reached her ankles in several places, she approached the sound. For every ten steps she stopped to listen and if necessary adjust her course. The moment the circle of light from the carbide lamp caught the dark rock, she knew she had fulfilled her side of the contract. The rock was of the same gray-black color as the small, quivering stone in her pocket. It looked like the nose of a submarine that had forced its way up through the floor of the cave. The humming was now very noticeable. She placed her hands on the rock, but to her amazement felt no quivering. Prompted by the text on the first note, she slowly put her ear to the rock, but she was still shocked when the deafening thunder erupted. She carefully approached the stone with her other ear and repeated Josef Siedler's 1907 experience of temporary deafness and the four howling tones.

As her deafness subsided, she found the tape recorder. The peak-meter reacted to the constant humming and went off the scale immediately when the microphone came into physical contact with the rock. She attached the sensors of the vibra-meter to the rock, but they detected nothing. As she packed away her apparatus, she noticed that the water level had started to rise. It was the dreaded siphon, but she got out in time, soaked up to her hips. Wearing wet trousers during her long trek out of Hölloch gave her a massive cold that killed four people the next day, including herself. On a motorway junction near Karlsruhe, she was surprised by a sudden sneeze and hit a car with a young family. The limited media attention allocated to the car crash focused on the two dead children.

Nine years later, when Ulrike's successor at the museum—the present author—came across the descriptive inventory of *Central European Mystery* in the archives and discovered that there was no corresponding artifact in the museum's collection, the cause of her death was partly reconstructed.

ABOUT THE AUTHOR

Peter Adolphsen was born in 1972 and attended the Danish Writers' School from 1993 to 1995. At twenty-five, he made his debut as an author with a collection of short prose entitled *Small Stories*, followed in 2000 by *Small Stories 2*. His novel *Machine* was published in English in 2008.

ABOUT THE TRANSLATOR

Photo copyright John Henderson, 2011.

Charlotte Barslund is a Scandinavian translator. She has translated novels by Karin Fossum, Per Petterson, Carsten Jensen, Sissel-Jo Gazan, Thomas Enger, and Mikkel Birkegaard as well as a wide range of classic and contemporary plays. She translated Peter Adolphsen's *Machine* in 2008.